EDEN

EDEN

Samantha Pegues

ISBN: 978-0-5786-6755-3

Published by Pegues Enterprises

www.samanthapegues.org

DEDICATION

This novel is dedicated to children of all races. I pray that you come forth with boldness, wisdom, knowledge, love and kindness, without racism, prejudices and hatred and turn the world around.

I also dedicate this book to every leader. May God give you strength, courage and conviction to serve the people without discrimination and malice. You will serve with honor, compassion and wisdom.

CHAPTER 1

*I*t was a beautiful, summer day. The Clifton family was on an airplane, headed back to the United States from their vacation in Israel.

It was Kennedi Clifton's first time riding in a commercial airplane. She was anxious, but excited.

She had met three amazing, new friends while in Israel - Kyle from North Korea, Jaxson from Russia, and Faith from China.

Their parents, who worked for the government, had an important, secret meeting to attend, so they left their children in their seats and went to a secret cabin in the plane. After more than hour, Jaxson said, "Our parents have been gone for a long time. I think we should go check on them."

"I think that's a good idea," Kennedi replied. "Besides, I would love to tour the plane, considering I'm a virgin to flying commercially.

Faith laughed. "Are you serious?"

"Well, yeah, kind of," Kennedy said. "We normally take my mom's private jet. She says it's for my safety. I thought it was strange when we didn't take her jet back home."

They got up and started walking toward the back of the plane. They noticed that government officials were seated at the front. Those who seemed to be wealthy were in the next section. The middle class was next, and the lower class was at the very back of plane. The people at the back were partying and talking loudly. They weren't paying attention to what was going on around them.

"Hey, guys. I wonder what's behind this door." Faith said.

They slowly cracked open the door. They saw world leaders sitting around a table, and the more they listened, the more apparent it became that they were planning a war.

On a huge screen, there were images demonstrating a plummeting economy like boarded-up windows, unemployment lines, and tanking stock market numbers. On the screen flashed terms like "record unemployment", "food shortage", and "evictions and foreclosures skyrocketing". The images flashing on the screen were shocking, but what was even more disturbing to them was that the leaders were apparently laughing at it all; enjoying it.

"How could they laugh at something that could hurt so many people?" Kyle asked.

"They must be planning this for the future," Kennedi said. "We must find a way to stop them!"

"We can't tell anyone what we've seen," Jaxson said. "Let's go back to our seats and we'll figure out something after we land."

They were headed back to their seats when the plane suddenly began to descend.

"Sit down, now!" the stewardess yelled.

They all had to take a seat at the rear of the plane because they didn't have time to return to the front.

Before the plane could come to a complete stop, a man at the front grabbed his backpack and ran off the plane.

"Who the heck was that? Dude has lost his freaking mind!" Kyle said.

"Oh, snap! Dude, that was the former president. What the hell is he doing?" Jaxson asked.

Moments later, they arrived at the Memphis International Airport.

"Look!" Faith shouted. "They've built a tunnel on the side of the airport. I wonder what that's for? It wasn't there the last time my family was here."

"Sections one and two, please gather your belongings and quickly exit the plane," the stewardess announced.

Government officials and the wealthy folks quickly exited.

"Your attention, please," the stewardess said. "The rest of you will exit on the right side of the plane, through the emergency exit. Follow the instructions of the outside personnel. Thank you."

"I don't like the sound of this," Faith said slowly.

As they exited the plane, they were forced to enter the tunnel. It led to an enormous, fenced-in area. The fence was topped with what appeared to be sharp razors.

"This isn't right," Kennedi said under her breath. "Where are our parents?"

As they exited the plane and entered the fenced area, they noticed that many children were separated from their parents. After a short period of time had passed, the voice of the former President came onto an intercom and said, "America, this is it. God doesn't decide when the end of the world will be – the government does. A bomb has been planted. All of you will die in twenty minutes. Farewell. God bless."

The huge plane they were riding on took off. Drones appeared out of thin air and began shooting. The sky appeared to be raining down fire. The people were left to die.

The plane cabin erupted into chaos. Some ran, as if there was anywhere to go. Others yelled but their words only added to the din and panic. Some just sat, crying and praying. A few just laid down to die, helpless and hopeless, waiting for the end.

"Guys, we have to find the bomb and deactivate it," Kyle said. "Faith, you go east. Jaxson, you go west. Kennedi, you go south, and I'll take north. We'll meet back up at this spot in ten minutes."

After a quick but thorough search, they were unable to locate the bomb. One by one, they regrouped where they started.

Kennedi began to cry. "What do we do now?"

"Guys, I understand your frustration, but we can't give up. We must stay focused. Let's hold hands and pray," Faith suggested.

When they all held hands, something amazing happened - their appearances and even their attire changed. A shield appeared in Faith's hand. Kyle received a shiny, eye-catching belt. Jaxson got a cool vest. And a sparkling pair of shoes appeared on Kennedi's feet.

"Wow!" Faith yelled.

"We'll figure out what this means later. We have a bomb to find! Stay focused!" Kyle shouted.

Immediately, Kennedi's shoes lit up and started pulling her feet. Unintentionally, she began to run at an incredible speed. The others followed her. She came to an immediate stop at the edge of a small cliff. The others caught up one by one and joined her.

"Now what?" Jaxson asked. "This must mean something."

Faith pointed and yelled, "Look over there! There's the bomb!"

The bomb was partially obscured by brush someone had piled on top of it. They ran over to it and cleared it away.

"Does anyone know how to deactivate it? Kennedi asked.

"Google it!" Faith yelled.

"I got it!" Kyle shouted.

"Hurry! We only have seven seconds!" Kennedi shouted.

"Pull the yellow and blue wires at the same time," Kyle said.

Jaxson gritted his teeth, closed his eyes, and pulled the wires. The bomb was deactivated. After a moment of stunned silence, they all leapt with joy and hugged each other.

CHAPTER 2

"So what do we do now?" Kennedi asked. "The bomb is disarmed but we still have no food, water, or shelter. The drones burned most of our land and we're now stranded."

"Man, we don't even have a McDonalds!" Kyle shouted.

Everyone laughed.

"Maybe that's a good thing," Kyle chuckled.

Faith interrupted, "Look on the bright side - at least we now have the power to build our own society that's free of racism, prejudices, greed and hatred."

First, we need to announce to everyone that the bomb has been deactivated.

"Jaxson, I think you should do it," Kennedi suggested.

"Yeah, Jaxson. You're a great spokesperson," Faith added.

"Okay. Come on, let's go," Jaxson said.

Jaxson whistled and yelled, "People, listen up! We've deactivated the bomb. You're all safe."

Everyone cheered and applauded.

"If we want to survive, we must all work together. We found a river. However, we must find food, and figure out how to purify the water. Does anyone have any suggestions?"

"Well, for right now, we can boil some water until we're able to figure out a purification system. My grandfather taught me how to start a fire," a civilian suggested.

"I have an apple!" a young boy yelled.

"I have some peanuts," a random lady shouted.

"I have some rice," another man said.

Everyone came together and shared the food they brought on the plane.

"Before we get carried away, we need to develop some type of governmental system. Without structure, we're all doomed," Faith said. "Raise your hand if you're in favor."

Everyone raised their hands.

"Let's start with the president and vice-president. Rule number one; there will be no political parties," Kennedi suggested. "They only magnify racism and prejudices. Many people say "democrats or republicans" but they really mean black or white, and poor or rich.

It just creates too much foolishness. All democrats aren't good, and all republicans aren't bad. We need to get to know people for who they are, and not judge them solely by the party they represent."

Jaxson added, "While we won't totally agree on every issue, we can still agree to disagree, and work together with respect and class. Despite popular belief, compromise is not a curse word. Neither is it a sign of weakness."

"So, who wants to run for president?" Kyle asked.

Two hands went up.

"Sir, what's your name, and what makes you qualified for this position?"

"My name is Dakota Natchez. What qualifies me for this position? I am the last Native American male left in my family. My dad's ancestors lived in Memphis, and my mom's ancestors were from Mississippi. We had our own agriculture and economy before my family was colonized and then killed. We didn't have sickness and violence like America has today. We learned to live in peace. No one knows this soil like us."

The second candidate interrupted, "I agree with Dakota. I withdraw from the race."

"Everyone, let's welcome our new president! President Dakota Natchez!" Kyle announced.

Everyone cheered and clapped.

"That was easy. Now, who wants to run for vice-president?" Faith said.

A brown-skinned lady raised her hand.

"Ma'am, what's your name, and what qualifies you for this position?"

"I'm honest. I'm a strategic planner and I have a degree in international economic affairs. I'm fair, tough-skinned, and I love people of all races. By the way, I'm Angela Gipson," she said with confidence and poise.

"Angela, since no one wants to run against you, you are officially our vice-president," Faith said.

"Any runners for secretary of state and treasurer?" Faith asked.

A male and a female raised their hands.

"President Dakota, it's your duty to appoint the secretary of state and treasurer."

President Dakota announced, "As president, I would like to appoint Maria Pineda as the secretary of state, and I appoint Kevin Shankle as our treasurer. I've known them for years here in Memphis and their characters and reputations are impeccable. I would also like to make one other announcement. No longer shall this city be called Memphis. From this day forward, it will be known as Eden."

CHAPTER 3

"Okay, guys, now that we have established leadership, we must follow their instructions," Jackson said.

"As president, my first agenda is to establish a safe food and water supply," President Natchez explained. "Memphis should have the safest water supply in America. We have what's called an aquifer system. My family has been taking care of it and protecting it for over two hundred years."

He looked around, then said, "Come over here. I'll show it to you." He walked a short distance away, knelt, scooped up some soil, and rubbed it between his fingers.

"Do you see this? The clay is extremely rich in natural minerals. It helps to purify the water."

"I'm hungry. What are we going to do about food?" Faith asked.

"It will take too long to grow food for all of us," Natchez replied. "Does anyone have any suggestions? How will we get the products we need?"

The vice-president quickly answered, "I'm already on top of it. The city has not been taking full advantage of its location. There should be more imports and exports taking place from the harbor. I have reached out to a couple of friends from Georgia, Florida and California. I have also contacted people in other countries. They will all travel by water and meet us at the harbor."

Everyone began to talk about the connections and resources they had in other states and countries. In time, ships began to bring machinery, cars, food, clothes, lumber, and other products and materials into the harbor.

"Now we will have everything we need. We will build houses, businesses, and hospitals from scratch. There will be no unhealthy fast food restaurants. We will focus on health," President Natchez said.

"We have a slight problem," Angela responded.

"What's the problem?" President Natchez asked.

"We don't have the right population to fulfill the jobs to get the economy up and rolling. They don't have the skill sets required to accomplish the various tasks. We're going to have to recruit people from other states," Angela said.

"No problem," Maria Pineda responded. "I know talented, skilled people in Puerto Rico who would love to come here to work."

"Great, Maria," President Natchez said. "Send me a list of their names and dates of birth so we can run background checks first. If they pass them, I will send a ship to pick them up and bring them here. Please let them know that they will have to pass a health screening before entering our land and becoming a citizen of Eden."

After some time had passed, ships began to bring talented, wealthy people from other states to boost the economy. They built communities, shopping centers, restaurants, nightclubs, and stadiums for entertainment and sports.

CHAPTER 4

"*G*uys, are we just going to ignore what happened when we all joined hands? We must figure out what it means," Jaxson asked.

"What should we do?" Kyle asked.

"We have to join hands again," Kennedi replied.

"But what if something crazy happens?" Faith asked.

"There's only one way to find out," Jaxson said.

"No!" Kennedi yelled. "We'll figure this out later. We can't forget what we saw on the plane with our parents."

"Have any of your parents reached out to you?" Jaxson asked the group.

"No," Kennedi replied.

Faith and Kyle also said no.

"Maybe they think we're dead?" Faith questioned.

"We need get to Washington, D.C., now!" Kennedi shouted.

"Let's go tell President Natchez what's going on. Maybe he can give us some advice," Jaxson suggested.

They found the president and told them about all they had seen on the plane.

"What you saw has been in the works for many years, before your parents were elected. That's why you must be careful when seeking certain positions. You just might find yourself in the middle of something you didn't sign up for," President Natchez explained.

He immediately arranged a private flight to DC for them.

CHAPTER 5

*U*pon arrival in DC, they took a cab to Kennedi's mom's house. On the way, they saw a group of protesters. One of the protestor's signs read, "Give us back the 15th Amendment."

"What does the 15th Amendment address? The right to have a gun?" Kyle asked.

"No," Faith responded. "It gives all races the right to vote."

"Oh, wow," Jaxson said. "I wish there was something we could do."

"I can't drive any further. All of the streets are blocked off because of the protest," the driver stated.

"No problem," Kennedi responded. "We can walk to my mom's house from here. Here's a tip. Thank you so much."

Kennedi handed the driver a $20 bill. He thanked her.

"Let's go guys. We need to stop by my mom's house to see if she's there. She has some explaining to do," Kennedi said.

They fought their way through all of the protestors and arrived at Kennedi's house.

"Wow! Your house is beautiful!" Faith said.

"Shhhhh," Kennedi said quietly as she pointed toward the door.

Kennedi's mom, Mallory, was having a loud discussion with someone on the phone.

"Why isn't Trombley dead?" she shouted.

"I couldn't get a good shot," the man on the phone responded.

"You stupid idiot! You can't do anything right! We must take Trombley out tonight. Since the government won't impeach him, we must kill him before we go to war. The war will only prolong his presidency! You know what - never mind. I don't even know why I'm wasting my breath talking to you. I can't depend on you to do anything. I will do it myself. Give me my freaking money back!"

Mallory violently hung up the phone. Kennedi opened the door and her mom jumped back with a startled look on her face.

Playing dumb, Kennedi said, "Mom, next time, you should make sure the door is locked. Is everything okay? You seem very agitated. Who were you talking to?"

"Um, uh . . . just a coworker," Mallory replied. "Baby, give me a hug! I'm so glad you're okay!"

"Mama, why didn't you come looking for me? Why didn't you call?" Kennedi angrily replied.

"I-I thought you were dead, honey," Mallory stuttered.

Unable to hold in her anger any longer, Kennedi snapped, "You have always cared more about your job and money than me! I can't believe you! You want to be the president so badly; you would forsake your own flesh and blood; your own child. You would even kill for power. Shame on you! That's what's wrong with your generation. You've been corrupted by greed and power!"

"Kennedi Nicole! Don't you dare talk to me like that! I am your mother!" Mallory shouted.

"Well, you don't act like it," Kennedi replied.

"What did you say, little girl? Say it again. I will beat your a—."

Faith interrupted. "Hi, Mrs. Clifton. Nice to meet you."

"Yeah, whatever," Mallory rudely responded.

"Kennedi, Google Memphis and see why I thought you were dead," Mallory said.

Kennedi followed her mom's instructions. When she Googled Memphis, a link from CNN popped up that read *Memphis destroyed. No survivors recorded.*

"Clearly, that is fake news. No one came to see if there were any survivors. The plan to depopulate us failed," Jaxson said.

"Now excuse me. I have a gala to attend. You and your little friends better

not mess up my house while I'm gone,"
Mallory warned them. Then she rolled
her eyes and stormed out the door.

CHAPTER 6

"I don't trust her," Kennedi said, pacing back and forth.

"Kennedi, may I ask a question? Are you adopted?" Jaxson asked.

"Why do you ask?" Kennedi replied.

"Well, your mom is white but you're black. Something has to be going on," Jaxson responded.

"No, silly. My dad is black," Kennedi laughingly replied.

She walked over to a painting on the wall. She removed it and opened a safe located inside of the wall.

"Oh, no! It's gone!" Kennedi shouted in shock.

"What's gone?" Kyle asked.

"My mom's gun!" Kennedi replied. "We have to find out what gala she's going to. Now!"

They left the house. As soon as they walked into the breezeway, a man dressed completely in white stepped in front of them, blocking their path.

"Uh, excuse me, sir," Faith said.

"Going somewhere?" the man asked.

"Yes. Who are you?" Kennedi asked. "I've never seen you before."

"Oh, really? Well, maybe you should be more observant. I've seen you several times, Kennedi."

"Wait, how do you know my name?" Kennedi asked.

"I know all of your names." Pointing at each of them, he continued, "You're Faith. You're Jaxson. What's up, Kyle?"

"Man, you don't know me. Who told you my name? I'm not even from America. What are you, some kind of spy?" Kyle asked.

"Well, don't you want to know my name?" the man asked.

"Okay, what's your name?" Jaxson asked.

"I'm Gabriel, but you can call me Gabe. Come into my place. Let me show you something."

"I don't know about this. You seem kind of creepy," Jaxson said slowly.

Gabe laughed and said, "Let me explain my relationship to you. The older generation would call me a guardian angel, or a prophet."

"Angel? Angels aren't real," Kyle interrupted.

"If you say so. You can say I'm kind of a cosmic Siri. I've been sent to give you a message and instructions. It's not a coincidence that you all met on the plane," Gabe explained.

Faith asked, "How do you know that?"

"Oh, Faith, why are you so full of doubt?" Gabe responded.

Faith looked at Gabriel in shock.

"The four of you have been chosen to bring peace to the world and to stop World War III before it happens prematurely," Gabe added.

They all looked at each other in awe.

"Man can cause things to happen too soon," Gabe explained.

"Why should we believe you?" Kennedi asked.

Gabe laughed and asked, "Why do you think you transform when you hold hands?"

They looked at each other and gasped. Gabe laughed again.

"Hold hands. Let me show you something," Gabe instructed.

They took each other's hands and immediately transformed into superheroes.

"Kennedi, your shoes represent peace. You have the ability to bring calm to chaotic situations," Gabe explained.

Gabe laughed and said, "Kyle, that's a pretty cool belt you got there, buddy. Where'd you get it?"

"There's a button on the right side of the buckle. It has the power to cause people to tell the truth; even when they're trying to tell a lie. It's called the Belt of Truth," Gabe explained.

"Faith, your shield is a supernatural magnifying glass. Hold it up. Let me show you," Gabe said.

Faith held up the shield as he instructed.

"Look, this is China. This is Israel. This is Iran. The shield gives you the ability to see trouble near and far so that you all can work together to prevent unnecessary violence and innocent bloodshed."

"Wow!" Faith yelled. "This is awesome!"

"It's called the Shield of Faith," Gabe said.

It's named after me? That's even more cool!"

"Last but not least . . . Jaxson!" Gabe said.

"Your power is within your chest. You are pure in heart. Your strongest gift is that you love unconditionally. You love people regardless of race or financial status. Love is the only power that's stronger than hate. Your breastplate is called the Breastplate of Righteousness. You have the power to cause hateful people to love," Gabe explained.

"So, did anyone have a vision when you held hands?" he asked.

They all clasped their hands together again.

Suddenly, they all transformed again. However, this time, Kennedi saw a troubling vision.

"I saw a vision of me sitting in what seemed to be a large stadium," Kennedi explained. "I felt extreme sadness. I saw a crowd of people walking in. They were all dressed in black. Then, I saw a casket with the United States' flag laying across it, which means a government official died. There was a lady with golden hair walking beside the casket. She stood out because she had on a peach-colored dress, while everyone else was dressed in black. I felt as if she was responsible for the death of whomever was in that casket. I yelled, 'Hey, I know you did this!' She turned her head toward me, but she had no face! I didn't care. I wasn't afraid. I ran toward her, but the policemen wouldn't allow me to get close to her."

Kyle said, "Wow, Kennedi! I had a vision too! I saw a map. People dressed in army uniforms rose up from the map and began to march all across the world. I heard the words 'changing of the guard'. They were all wearing masks. People from every state were wearing masks as they changed states."

Faith said, "My vision was similar to yours, Kyle. I saw a map of the United States. There were four cannons pointed toward it. Four nations were planning to attack America."

"Well, guys, my vision was much different. In fact, it was kind of awkward," Jaxson interjected.

"In my vision, I saw four ravens on the ground, eating bread. An eagle landed in front of the ravens. The eagle walked over to the ravens and tried to eat their bread. However, the ravens attacked the eagle and wouldn't allow it to eat. Does anyone know what that means?" Faith asked.

"First of all, it is out of character for an eagle to eat bread from the ground," Gabe stated. "The fact that it came to the ground to eat with birds it doesn't normally associate with is a sign of a shortage of food. This simply means there will be an attack on America's food supply. America will begin to operate in uncommon ways. Other countries are seeking to dismantle America and bring it to the ground. We must intercede on behalf of this country."

CHAPTER 7

"*O*h, my God! I think the faceless woman in the peach dress in my vision is my mom!" Kennedi shouted.

"Wow! She was wearing an ugly peach dress when she left!"

Kennedi gave her a look and Faith quickly added, "No offense."

"Gabe, do you know where the gala is that my mom is going to tonight? I think she's up to something terrible. We have to stop her!" Kennedi explained.

Gabe responded, "Yes, the address is 1600 Pennsylvania Ave. The party starts at seven. Here are four tickets." Gabe handed the tickets to Kennedi.

"Thanks, Gabe. We really appreciate your help."

"Uh, we can't go to the gala looking like this. Where can we find clothes?" Jaxson asked.

Gabe walked over to his enormous closet and pulled the doors open.

"Sheesh!" Faith said. "I guess you really are an angel! This closet is huge!"

"Gabe, you rock!" Kyle shouted.

They chose their attire and looked in the mirror, then Faith said, "Guys, I think we're ready to party."

CHAPTER 8

"*O*kay, guys. If you're ready to go, I'll drop you off," Gabe said. "Let me go around back and get the car. Lock the door. I'll meet you out front."

A shiny, spotless, platinum car with tinted windows slowly came around the corner.

"Wow! Check out Gabe's ride!" Jaxson shouted as he ran toward the car.

"Man, what do you do for a living? Are you a drug dealer?" Kyle asked jokingly.

"Are you a doctor?" Kennedi asked.

"A lawyer? Faith asked.

"A pimp?" Jaxson asked.

They all laughed and got into Gabe's custom-made Rolls Royce.

"Shhh!" Gabe said. "Trina, take us to 1600 Pennsylvania Avenue."

The car responded, "I sure will, Gabe. But first, I need Faith, Kennedi, Kyle, and Jaxson to fasten their seatbelts. Welcome aboard, guys. My name is Trina. I am your chauffeur for today. Enjoy your ride."

"Who in the heck was that?" Jaxson asked, shocked.

Gabe laughed and said, "Oh, that's my car. I named her Trina."

The ride in Gabe's car was short-lived but exhilarating. They were all amused but a little frightened too because they had never seen a car that talked and was independently driven.

When they reached their destination, the car parked itself.

"You have reached your destination. Please gather all your belongings and exit from the right side of the car to avoid traffic. Have an amazing day," Trina said.

"Thanks, Trina," they all said simultaneously.

"I don't know if I'm cut out for this lifestyle," Kyle said.

"I know, right?" Jaxson responded. "I feel crazy talking to a car."

Before the door closed, Gabe said, "Guys, enjoy yourselves but be very careful. Remember, you must use your powers from within to accomplish this task. I will be waiting to hear from you. Good luck!"

They confidently strolled up to the door of the building where the gala was taking place.

"May I have your tickets?" the man at the door asked.

"Sure," Kennedi responded, handing him four tickets.

"Thank you. Right this way," the man replied, motioning with his hand.

They walked into the gala. The room was covered with the finest, elaborate decorations.

"Yo, do you see this?" Kyle said loudly.

Jaxson secretly nudged Kyle and whispered, "Dude, calm down. Stop acting like you're from the hood. You're gonna get us caught. We have to act like we belong here. But yo, this is some cool stuff."

They laughed and continued to walk and look around. Most people were standing in groups, drinking wine and champagne. Others were sitting and enjoying hors d'oeuvres.

Kyle and Jaxson were approached by a handsome gentleman.

"Hi, I'm..."

"You're Reginald Clayton, the governor of Mississippi," Kennedi interrupted. "So... what are you going to do about the state of the prison system in your state? What plan do you have in place to decrease the number of deaths; especially those pertaining to inmates killing other inmates?"

"Well, right now..." Reginald began to explain.

Kennedi interrupted again, "Did you know about the inhumane living conditions in the prison system before the inmates began to expose it on social media?

Why are they being allowed to live with mold and no hot water?"

Reginal tried to interject but Kennedi continued.

"Speaking of water. Why is the water brown? Is this the same water that their meals are being prepared with? What type of healthcare are they receiving?"

"Ma'am, I can't answer your questions if you keep interrupting me," Reginald politely said.

"Never mind, Governor. We'll discuss this when we have more time. Have you seen my mom?"

Governor Clayton laughingly asked, "Who are you? What is your mom's name?"

"I am Kennedi Clifton, daughter of the secretary of state," Kennedi responded with confidence.

Governor Clayton took a deep breath and said, "That explains it. I should have known. You are just like your mom."

"And what does that mean?" Kennedi asked, folding her arms and giving the governor a mean stare.

"Oh, never mind. No, I haven't seen Mallory tonight. Now, please excuse me. I'm going to entertain a more pleasant conversation."

Governor Clayton walked away, shaking his head.

"My mom has to be here somewhere." Kennedi said. "There's no way we can get past security to the secret chambers of the building."

"Maybe there is," Faith replied. "We have to hold hands."

"We can't do that here in front of everyone," Jaxson said. "Let's find a more secluded area."

They left the main area and proceeded down a long hallway, only to find that there were several people there.

"I wonder what's downstairs?" Faith asked.

"I don't know. Let's check it out," Kennedi replied.

They proceeded to walk casually past the group, hoping they wouldn't be noticed.

"Hey! Where do you think you're going?" a police officer shouted.

"Sir, we're just trying to find the restroom. Can you help us out?" Jaxson responded.

"This area is only for White House personnel, but I will let you use the bathroom this time," the officer said.

"Thank you so much," Kennedi replied.

"Yeah, sure. Go around the corner and the bathroom is on the left. Use the bathroom and come straight back. Do not touch anything or I might have to kill you," the officer stated less than half-jokingly.

The walls of the restroom were covered with gold-veined, blue marble. The floors sparkled with diamonds that were meticulously embedded in them.

"Wow! This is amazing! I've never peed in a gold toilet before," Jaxson said, laughing with excitement.

Everyone laughed except Kennedi.

"Kennedi, are you okay? You look like you've seen a ghost. Who is it? Lincoln? Washington?"

Everyone laughed again until they realized Kennedi really was worried about something.

"Kennedi, what is it?" Kyle said.

"This looks familiar to me," Kennedi slowly responded. "I think I remember coming here when I was a child."

Kennedi began to pace back and forth. She appeared to be looking for something.

"Kennedi, will you please tell us what's going on?" Jaxson asked.

"Give me a second. I'm trying to figure out why I feel as if I've been here before," Kennedi explained.

"I thought you said this was your first time here?" Kyle asked.

"I didn't think I had been here, but this area has triggered something in my memory. Let's hold hands," Kennedi responded.

They did so and were immediately transformed into their superhero gear.

"I knew it!" Kennedi shouted. Remembering where she was, she immediately spoke more softly. "I *have* been here before! There is a door behind this wall that leads to an underground bunker. The president and his staff use it when there's a safety threat to the White House."

"Wow! How did you know that?" Jaxson asked.

"My mom brought me here when I was a little girl," Kennedi explained. "Come on, let's check it out!"

They entered through the hidden door and carefully tiptoed down the long, winding stairwell. As soon as they reached the bottom of the staircase, they heard a female's voice shouting profanities.

"That's my mom," Kennedi whispered. She held one finger to her lips and said, "Shhh." The others quieted down.

"Follow my lead."

"Oh my God! Look!" Faith whispered as she pointed at Kennedi's shoes. "Your shoes have light and fire coming from them again!"

Kennedi grabbed Faith's hand. "Hold my hand, guys! Let's go!" The others linked hands and held on tight. Suddenly, Kennedi began to run involuntarily, pulling them along with her until she came to a sudden halt, causing the others to bump into her.

"I don't know if I'll ever get used to that," Kennedi said, flustered. "Where are we?"

"Something significant has to be here – something we can't see with our eyes," Faith said, lifting up her shield. As she did so, they were all immediately able to see behind the wall. The president was tied to a chair with his mouth taped shut while Mallory held a gun to his head.

"We have to go in and stop her! Now!" Kennedi yelled.

"No! If she was going to shoot him, she would've done it by now. She obviously wants information of some kind from him. Let's see what she's up to," Faith suggested.

They quietly opened the door and slowly crept alongside the wall. They saw Mallory forcefully rip duct tape from the president's mouth.

"Ouch! You stupid piece of..." the president yelled before Mallory interrupted.

"Say it and I'll blow your ignorant brains out! If you want to live, you better do exactly as I say. I'm about to go live on all media platforms, and you better read exactly what's on these cue cards. Do you understand me?"

President Trombley gave Mallory a sarcastic look and nodded his head to confirm. Mallory violently slapped him on the back of the head and shouted, "Don't get quiet on me now! You've been running your big, egotistical mouth to the press and trying to expose us for months. I don't care about your title. You are a puppet. That's all you'll ever be to me. Now, read these cards!"

Mallory pressed the live button on President Trombley's phone. He began to read.

"Good evening, America. I'm coming to you live to report that we have been made aware of a virus that has possibly entered our country. But don't panic. Continue your normal lives. We've got it under control."

"I'll be reaching out to China," he continued. Off-camera, Mallory pointed her Glock at him and whispered, "Stick to the script or I'm gonna kill you."

"Well, that's all for now. I have a hair appointment that I have to get to," the President concluded. Mallory ended the video and screamed, "Do you think this is a game?" She then struck him across the back of the head with her pistol. Kennedi couldn't believe what she was seeing. They couldn't wait any longer. They burst into the room.

"Mama, what are you doing?" Kennedi yelled, tears racing down her cheeks.

"Kennedi? What the – what are you doing here?" Mallory asked, shocked to her core to see her daughter.

"I should be asking you the same thing. I can't believe you. I see why dad left. You are evil!" Kennedi began to cry uncontrollably.

"Baby, I can explain," Mallory pleaded, rushing to Kennedi and trying to hug her.

"Get away from me before I call the police!" Kennedi demanded.

"Come on, President Trombley. You're coming with us. We'll keep you safe." Kennedi looked at her mom and shook her head, the look on her face saying all she could not, a look that told Mallory there was no way to ever recover from this betrayal.

They secretly exited the White House. Kennedi called Gabe and explained what happened. Gabe quickly picked them up from President Trombley's secret, emergency hideout location.

"Nice to meet you, Mr. President," Gabe said, extending his hand.

"Who the heck are you?" President Trombley asked.

"I'll explain later, but right now, just consider me your guardian angel," Gabe responded, chuckling slightly.

"Mission accomplished," Kennedi said as she gave the other a high-five, but her joy quickly returned to sorrow, knowing that in saving the president, she had become an emotional orphan.

CHAPTER 9

They returned to Eden with President Trombley. Upon arrival, the president was told that he had to undergo a medical exam before entering the community.

"What? I'm the President. You can't test me! I make the rules!" Trombley exclaimed.

"You don't make the rules here," President Natchez replied. "I do. If you don't like our laws, feel free to return to DC and get killed."

"Who are you?" Trombley asked.

"I'm Dakota Natchez, President of Eden."

"Whatever. What does the exam consist of?" Trombley asked.

"We simply check your temperature and your blood," President Natchez responded. We don't require any vaccinations. However, you seem to be mentally exhausted, so you will also be required to undergo a psychological evaluation."

"Whatever you say, man. Let's just get this over with," Trombley said.

Trombley was escorted to the medical center for an evaluation.

"Who had the vision about the people walking across the map wearing masks that covered the lower portion of their faces?" Gabe asked.

"That would be me," Kyle responded. "It was quite strange. They all had tight eyes, as if they were from my native country."

"Hey, didn't President Trombley mention something about China and a virus before your mom cut him off?" Faith asked Kennedi.

"Yes. Let's pay him a visit and ask him what he knows," Kennedi responded.

"Gabe, come with us," Jaxson said.

They went to the medical center to speak to President Trombley. They found him resting in bed while classical music softly played in the background.

"President Trombley," Kyle whispered softly.

The president slowly opened his eyes, became startled, then realized where he was. "Man, I didn't realize I was that tired. What's going on?"

"Do you know anything about a group of people who are walking around wearing masks?" Kyle asked.

"Yes. People all over America and the world are wearing masks now."

"Not in North Korea, they're weren't!" Kyle said, stunned.

"Well, North Korea is an alternate reality. But why isn't anyone here wearing one? You guys are going to get infected! Oh my God! Get away from me! Find me a mask!"

President Trombley pushed the panic button on his bead. Dr. Nisha Davis raced into the room.

"What's going on?" she asked.

"I need a mask! Get me a mask now!" Trombley demanded.

Dr. Davis took a deep breath and responded in a gentle but sarcastic manner.

"First of all, that isn't the proper way to ask for anything. I'm going to need you to adjust your tone and intelligently communicate your needs," Dr. Davis said.

"Why don't you people have on masks?" Trombley asked in a nicer tone.

Dr. Davis looked into his eyes and sternly asked, "What do you mean by *you people*?"

"I apologize. Let me rephrase the question. Why is no one in this city wearing a mask?" Trombley asked.

"Why *should* we have on masks?" Dr. Davis replied.

"Haven't you heard about the virus?"

"No. What virus are you talking about?"

"Corisis. It has killed thousands of people in America and other countries. Haven't you heard about it?"

"No. Whatever that virus is, it's nonexistent here," Dr. Davis responded. "Y'all need to keep that mess away from us. Where was the nova?

"China. By the time they notified us, it had already spread to other countries. Our administration simply wasn't prepared to handle the severity of it with such short notice," Trombley explained.

"Hmm. I sense there's a lot more to it than that," Faith said.

"Watch LNN. You'll see what I'm talking about," Trombley suggested.

"Oh, heck no," Dr. Davis responded. "We don't watch that when we want the truth. L-N-N, the Lying News Network."

Dr. Davis turned to Faith and added, "Faith, you're right. There is more to it than what he's telling us. We're going to need your shield to figure this one out. Hold hands, guys."

Faith, Kennedi, Jaxson, and Kyle held hands and transformed. Faith held up her shield. Immediately, New York City popped up.

"Oh, my God! This is exactly what I saw in my vision. Everyone was wearing masks. And the shelves in the grocery stores were empty," Kyle proclaimed.

"Shift to another state. Let's see what else is going on," Faith suggested.

"Yeah, let's see if the people are still protesting in DC," Jaxson said.

Faith programmed her shield for Washington, D.C. Masked policemen and the National Guard were attempting to calm outraged citizens who were looting, burning buildings, and destroying police vehicles.

"No way! I wonder what fueled all of this?" Kyle asked.

"Guys, check this out. I Googled it. It appears that another unarmed black man was killed by a white police officer," Kennedi sadly explained.

"When is it going to end?" Jaxson asked.

"We are the generation who will have to make a difference. We don't care about race, power, or greed. History and the cares of life have caused the older generation's hearts to become cold and unforgiving," Faith explained.

"So, Mr. Trombley? What are you going to do about this?" President Natchez asked.

"It's terrible what happened to the gentleman. I will demand an immediate investigation," Trombley replied.

"Investigation? Why is it that police officers get an investigation before they're arrested but civilians don't?" President Natchez asked. "They are supposed to enforce the laws, not be above them. Criminals belong in jail, not in coffins."

"Look, don't ask me questions like that," Trombley responded. Those laws were in place long before I was elected into office. You can't blame this one on me."

"You may not have written the laws, but you can use your power to change them," President Natchez argued.

"Trombley, what else do you know about the riots?" Faith asked.

"What do you mean, what do I know about it?" Trombley snapped. "I have the same info that you have. I'm not out there in the streets with them."

Jaxson pressed the button on his breastplate and asked, "What did you say, Mr. Trombley?"

"Police officers have increased inhumane practices against minorities. The elite knows that they will burn down their communities and will not be able to afford to restore them. Wealthy investors will buy their communities and push them out. Police violence will increase, and it will be suggested that the police be removed, then military forces will move in. This will be the beginning of a one-world government. There is a hidden agenda behind all of the madness."

Trombley quickly put his hand over his mouth, then asked, "What just happened? What have you done to me?"

"That is just evil," President Natchez said. It seems like you guys are trying to create a race war to enforce martial law, which would mean that restrictions will be placed on the second and fifteenth amendments."

"Hmm. Isn't this an election year? That would also mean that you would continue to be the president for four more years," Kennedi said as she gave Mr. Trombley a suspicious look.

Trombley dropped his head and didn't respond.

"You're gonna have to deal with that. We have to figure out what's going on with this virus. Faith, use your shield to scan China," Dr. Davis commanded.

Faith programmed her shield to view China. They saw what appeared to be a doctor in a lab drawing blood from bats and placing it in tubes for coagulation. After a few minutes passed, he injected a rat with the blood that was drawn from the bat.

"Sick dog," Mr. Trombley said with disgust.

"Do you know him?" Dr. Davis asked.

"Yes, that's Dr. Yung," Mr. Trombley responded. "It was speculated that he created Corisis years ago to control the population in China."

"Well, it looks like you are about to reap what your ancestors have sown," President Natchez said, sighing and shaking his head.

"What do you mean by that?" Mr. Trombley asked.

"My ancestors didn't have much sickness or disease when your ancestors came onto our land," Natchez explained. "We ate clean and didn't practice sexual immorality. Your ancestors brought diseases and infected us, then they took over our land. It looks like the same thing is about to happen to you if you don't develop a strategy to stop it."

"I need a sample of what's in that lab so I can know exactly what we're dealing with," Dr. Davis stated. "You guys must go to China. Now!"

CHAPTER 10

*P*resident Natchez arranged for a private flight to China for the crew. Upon their arrival, they stopped at a hotel to rest from jet lag.

"Wow! Look at this!" Kennedi beamed.

The hotel was vastly different from American hotels. Robots were assisting guests with their luggage, and serving guests food in the dining area. There was no concierge at the front desk.

"How do we check in?" Jaxson asked.

"The concierge only assists when there's a problem. Look over there. We check-in through the human hologram," Kyle explained.

"Jesus Christ! How did you know that?" Jaxson asked.

"I eavesdrop on my dad's conversations all the time. This is the plan for the rest of the world too. It's just a matter of time," Kyle explained.

They slowly walked over to the hologram to check in. Her eyes blinked and she said, very politely, "Hi. Welcome to Illumination Palace. I'm Chen. How may I assist you?"

"We would like two rooms," Kyle replied.

"Please state the size and number of beds would you like, and how many nights will you be staying with us." Chen said.

"We would like king-size beds, and we'll be staying for two nights," Faith responded.

"Okay. We have a two-bedroom suite available for $795 per night," Chen said.

"What? Eight hundred dollars?" Jaxson asked.

"We'll take it!" Kennedi interjected.

"Great. Hold up your right hand," Chen suggested.

Kennedi lifted up her right hand. Blue beams shined from Chen's eyes and began to scan Kennedi's hand.

"You don't have a barcode. I cannot process your payment. Please proceed to the concierge's desk for human assistance. Have an amazing day!" Chen said cheerfully.

"Yo, this is freaking me out," Jaxson said. "I'm prepared for a different time zone, but not a different century. Sheesh!"

They proceeded to the front desk, where they were met by the hotel manager.

"Hello. My name is Kin. I hear you don't have money to pay," he said.

"We have plenty of money on our debit cards," Kyle said.

Kin laughed. "Debit card? You must be from America. Your country is way behind. We don't use debit cards here. Everything is digital."

"So, how will we pay for a room? We are not getting a chip, or barcode, or whatever you want to call it, inserted into our bodies," Janoon replied.

"You are rebellious, just like your president. The United States is behind on implementing a one world, one currency government. You will have no choice but to accept the chip as it will store all of your medical and financial data. Unless you have a chip, you won't be able to buy or sell anything. Tell your president that his time is running out. We already have other countries on board. America's economy can't stand alone. They need us. Give me your hand. I can insert the chip. You won't feel it. I will only take five seconds," Kin insisted.

"No!" Jaxson yelled.

"Guys, it can't be that bad. I'll do it," Kyle said, reaching out to Kin.

Out of nowhere, Gabe showed up and grabbed Kyle's hand. "I'll take care of this," Gabe said. "You can scan my chip.

Kin scanned Gabe's chip and gave them their room keys.

"Thank you, John," Kin said. Please place your bags on the cart and our bionic men will assist you to your rooms. Enjoy your day."

Two robots came, assisted them with their luggage, and showed them to their rooms.

"I've overheard my dad talking about all of this stuff, but I didn't quite understand it," Kyle said.

"Gabe, how did you know we were here? And who the heck is John?" Faith asked.

Gabe laughed and said, "I told you. I'm your guardian angel. I see you even when you don't see me."

"Why did you take the chip?" Kennedi asked.

"It's not a real chip," Gabe explained. "I discovered a way to trick their system so I can still operate in the world without submitting to the new normal. That's why the concierge called me John. The chip is filled with false information and I've encrypted it so my information cannot be altered. I've brought one for you as well. Although all of you are immune from the virus, your information can be altered through their system. This chip will prevent that."

"Thanks, John - I mean, Gabe," Jaxson said. Everyone laughed.

"You guys need to get some sleep. You have a long day ahead. You need your rest so you can focus," Gabe suggested.

They all said goodnight and went to bed.

CHAPTER 11

*G*abe slept in a separate suite. At around three a.m., he had a strange feeling of anxiety and fear. He ran and knocked on the teens' door. Faith opened it.

"What's going on , Gabe? We've barely had any sleep."

"You have to leave now!"

"What do you mean, leave now?" Jaxson asked, yawning and wiping his eyes.

"You must move now to catch Dr. Yung off-guard. He would never expect company at this hour."

They scrambled to get dressed as quickly as they could, and prepared to go to the lab to confront Dr. Yung.

"Here's the address." Gabe handed a business card to Faith. "When you get there, go to the alley on the left and go through the back door. Be careful."

They left the hotel and went to the lab. When they arrived, they followed Gabe's instructions.

"Check this out, guys," Jaxson said. "This door isn't locked."

They proceeded through the door and immediately heard chatter.

"I have made the virus stronger," an anonymous voice said. "The second wave wiped out more people and businesses than the first did. This will be the beginning of the end of the American economy."

"I wonder if that's Dr. Yung," Kyle asked.

"There's only one way to find out," Faith replied.

Jaxson entered the rear of the lab, saw Yung on the phone, and said, "Hello, Dr. Yung. Who are you talking to?"

Dr. Yung looked back, startled, began to speak Chinese, and hung up the phone. He pointed his finger at them and yelled, "Who are you? What do you want?"

"We want all of the vials of Corisis," Kennedi answered.

"I don't know what you're talking about," Dr. Yung responded.

"Really? So, what were you just saying? Who were you on the phone with?" Kyle asked.

"None of your business. Get out of my lab before I call the police!"

Kennedi laughed.

"You won't call the police, because if you do, you will go to jail," Kennedi said.

They all held hands and transformed. Dr. Yung gazed at them in fear.

Kyle pressed the button of truth and asked, "Where are the vials that contain the virus?"

"They are behind the glass," Dr. Yung involuntarily responded.

Faith walked over to the huge glass door. "Over here, guys!" she shouted.

They all turned and walked toward Faith. Dr. Yung picked up a scaffold and attempted to stab Jaxson.

"Jaxson, look out!" Faith yelled.

Jaxson quickly turned around and seized the scaffold from Dr. Yung, then twisted his arm behind his back and gently placed him on the ground.

"Dr. Yung, where are the missing vials?" Kennedi asked.

"Huh? My English not so good," Dr. Yung responded.

Jaxson twisted his arm a little tighter. "Okay!" he yelled. "I sent them to the United States to be replicated for the second wave," Dr. Yung continued.

"You did what?" Kyle shouted, pressing his truth button again.

"The virus will quickly spread throughout the world, especially America. They can't afford to keep their economy shut down. We will require Americans to be vaccinated before traveling. Many will be injected with the virus. America will lose many lives and economic power. Their time to reign is coming to an end. There shall be a change of the guard."

"You are one sick SOB. I should stick one of these up your..." Kyle said, holding the needle near Yung's skin.

"No! No! Please, my friend!" Dr. Yung pleaded.

"We would never stoop to your level, you sleazeball. Guys, box up those vials and let's go," Gabe said.

"Come on, Doc. You're coming with us," Kennedi said.

CHAPTER 12

*U*pon arrival in Eden, Dr. Yung was sent to Dr. Davis to undergo a health screening.

"Dr. Yung. You sick, cold-hearted bastard. How could you do this?" Mr. Trombley angrily asked.

"Hold on, Mr. Trombley," President Natchez interrupted. "You reap what you sow. Isn't that what the Bible says?"

"Yeah, what's your point?" Trombley answered sarcastically.

"Your ancestors came to America and were welcomed with open arms by my people. And they thanked them by killing them with diseases, or by outright murder when the diseases progressed too slowly for their liking. Still, there was no repentance. No mercy. They saw this genocide as a way to grab their land. Sound familiar? Life, liberty, and the pursuit of happiness only applied to themselves. You can't be mad at Dr. Yung for doing what he did unless you repent and apologize for what your ancestors did. Maybe we wouldn't be going through all of this mess if your ancestors had chosen to live peacefully with the Native Americans. If you live by the sword, by that same sword, you just might die."

Mr. Trombley was about to respond to President Natchez with a sarcastic comment, but Jaxson pressed the button on his chest.

"You are absolutely right," Trombley said, beginning to cry. "While I can't undo the damage that has already taken place, I can do everything in my power to make sure that it never happens again under my leadership." Trombley then gave President Natchez a hug.

As he comforted Trombley, President Natchez looked at Jaxson and said, "We need to find a way to mass produce that truth button. The world needs more honesty like this."

"Guys, let's give them a moment," Dr. Davis said.

"Here you go, Dr. Davis," Kyle said as he handed her the vials.

"Thanks, guys. Let me run some tests to see what kind of concoction this is and I'll let you know if we need a vaccination."

Dr. Davis then turned to Dr. Yung. "You need your butt whipped for this!" She punched Dr. Yung in the nose. He spun around and held his face as blood dripped through his fingers. Dr. Davis exited the room. Dr. Yung grabbed a cloth, held it to his nose, walked to a chair, and sat down with his head tilted back.

"Can't say he didn't deserve that," Gabe said to the teens. "While Dr. Davis is working on that, we need to focus on the next mission. Who had the vision about the missiles?"

"That would be me," replied Faith.

"Could you see where they were coming from?" Gabe inquired.

"Yes. Iran, Russia, China, and North Korea," Faith confirmed.

"I wonder if this somehow connected to what we saw on the plane? Do you think our parents have anything to do with this?" Kyle questioned.

"At this point, I wouldn't put anything past anyone. You saw what my mom did," Kennedi stated.

"Well, there's only one way to find out. Give me your parents' contact info," Gabe suggested.

They gave Gabe the requested information, and he used it to hack into all of their email and cell phone accounts.

"I hate to tell you this, but you guys were exactly right. Your parents definitely have their hands in this one," Gabe said solemnly.

"How do you know?" Kyle asked.

"I hacked into the apps on your parents' phones. Listen to this," Gabe replied.

"During the second wave of Corisis, America's economy will take a major hit. They will be consumed with racial tension and the virus. We can use this time to strike. It's time to change the guard. Who made them the god of the world? It's time to give them a taste of their own medicine."

"That's my dad's voice. I can't believe this. How were you able to retrieve those audio files?" Kyle asked.

"You know when you download apps to your phone and you're prompted to allow the app to access your photos and record your audio and videos? Apps can record all of your conversations and videos and store them. Hackers, like myself, can easily gain access to your entire life. Be careful," Gabe warned them.

They all looked at each other in shock.

Trying to lighten the mood, Gabe joked, "No worries. I won't tell your parents that you've been cursing."

"So, what do we do about their plan to attack us? How do we stop them?" Kennedi asked.

"There is no way to stop them because we cannot go to each country and destroy their weapons. Therefore, we must be prepared for them when they arrive on September fifteenth."

"President Trombley, you must return to the White House and notify the military. I deactivated the tracking device in your phone. Do not tell anyone where you've been," Dr. Davis commanded.

"Aren't all of you coming with me?" Trombley asked.

"No, we will be there on the fourteenth," Gabe responded.

"Tomorrow is the fourteenth of September, you know," Trombley said with a smirk on his face.

"Well, I guess we can go with you," Gabe responded.

"Make sure you tell the world that no vaccination is needed. We will just have to wait this one out. Quarantine, vitamin C, herbs, zinc and immune builders are the best defense right now," Dr. Davis explained to Trombley, handing him his phone.

Trombley started getting notifications back to back.

"Someone must be looking for you," Kennedi asked.

"No, check this out. I'm under fire for something I didn't even post," Trombley responded.

He handed his phone to Dr. Davis so she could see the news being broadcasted.

"There's no way you could've posted that because I've had your phone, and all of the apps' features were deactivated," Dr. Davis said.

"Man, you have too much drama," President Natchez said, shaking his head. "Let me arrange a private jet to take you back home. We don't need that drama over here."

CHAPTER 13

*U*pon his arrival at the capitol, President Trombley immediately called an emergency meeting with the military. Troops traveled in and brought food, water and other emergency necessities. They spent the entire day preparing the city and nation for an attack.

"Are you going to make a public announcement to notify the people about what's going on?" Jaxson asked President Trombley.

"Absolutely not. The other party will send this nation into chaos. They will lie, saying I planned an attack on my own country and troops. It will only be fuel for them to try to impeach me. I will simply tell them that we must go on lockdown for the second wave of Corisis."

After all of the troops were in place, President Trombley was taken to an underground bunker for safety. He allowed Gabe, Kennedi, Kyle, Faith, and Jaxson to stay the night with him for safety. At three a.m., Gabe awakened everyone.

"President Trombley! Wake up!" Gabe shouted. "You must tell the troops to get into position now!"

President Trombley obeyed Gabe's orders. Moments later, they heard a deafening noise that shook the ground, like thunder backed by a million trumpets.

"Guys, you must hold hands now!" Gabe instructed.

Kennedi, Kyle, Jaxson, and Faith held hands to activate their superpowers.

"We speak to the four winds from the North, South, East, and West. We command you to come forth in full force now!" Kyle shouted.

Immediately, a violent windstorm formed, capturing the four missiles that were headed toward America and casting them into the ocean. The combustion was brutally strong and caused a great flood.

"Whew!" That was scary!" Kyle screamed.

"What are you going to do about the flood you've caused? Can you use your superpowers to clean this up?" President Trombley asked.

They all laughed.

"What do you mean, what are we gonna do?" Kennedi asked. "This is your country. You're the president. You're going to have to figure this one out."

"I hope you didn't fire all of your staff, because you're going to need help with this one," Jaxson said.

"Yeah, we only came to help," Kyle added. "We have to get back to Eden. Good luck." He and the others headed to the plane to leave.

"Wait a minute!" President Trombley yelled, running after them. "I recognize that God's hands are upon you. Jaxson, did you have a vision?"

"Yes, I did. We've already solved my vision on our end. We just need you to follow suit. Come back to Eden with us and I'll tell you all about it," Jaxson replied.

They all boarded the private jet and headed back to Eden.

CHAPTER 14

"*I*n my vision, I saw four black crows eating bread," Jaxson said. "An eagle landed and tried to eat some of their bread. But the crows wouldn't allow it to eat. Do you know what that means, Mr. President?"

"No, I don't," President Trombley responded.

"Four nations shall rise up against you in an attempt to control America's food supply and money," Jaxson explained.

"It's out of character for an eagle to eat bread from the ground," Jaxson continued. "The eagle symbolizes America. The fall of America is being plotted as we speak. Follow me. Let me show you around."

Jaxson took President Trombley on a tour around Eden.

"We invest in agriculture," Jaxson elaborated. "We give our farmers bigger tax breaks, and we set aside land specifically for agriculture. We must go back to Genesis. Adam and Eve had everything they needed in the garden of Eden. However, their desire to have more knowledge than God resulted in their downfall. Sound familiar?"

"At Eden, we focus on health and safety," Jaxson continued. "Our fast food restaurants specialize in clean eating. We've developed our own automobile and textile industries. While our profit is less because we don't focus on outsourcing to foreign countries for cheap labor, we still make a profit. Greed and power have caused much turmoil amongst countries and people. When we value money more than human life, we eventually lose them both. At least we won't have to give other countries control over our products. We've also cultivated other relationships, especially with Canada, for the use of petroleum. While we should keep and develop positive business relationships with other countries, we should never set ourselves up to be controlled by anyone."

"You are a very intelligent young man," President Trombley said, patting Jaxson on the back.

"I think you are intelligent as well," Jaxson said. "Your childhood and life experiences caused your heart to become hard, but deep down inside, you are a good person. We most definitely have to work on how you relay your point of view to the masses. You were elected for one reason, but I believe God has a greater purpose for you. He's going to use you to stop America from becoming a communist nation. Here, I'm going to give you my heart. You're going to need it to give you the power to do what's best for the country."

He handed President Trombley a heart-shaped button. Tears raced down President Trombley's face.

Gabe, Kennedi, Kyle, Faith, President Natchez, and Dr. Davis approached President Trombley and Jaxson as they were talking.

"Just as our powers don't work unless we're together, this nation won't operate in its true power unless all races work together," Jaxon said. "A nation divided can't stand."

They all hugged. "Let's hold hands and pray," Dr. Davis suggested.

They all held hands as Jaxson prayed.

"Oh, my God! Look!" Jaxson shouted, pointing at President Trombley, who had transformed into a superhero.

"Thank you, God. I believe I just received the power I need to run the second lap in this race. Get ready, America."

President Trombley laughed.

To be continued . . .

CPSIA information can be obtained
at www.ICGtesting.com
Printed in the USA
LVHW041221080920
665326LV00004B/272